This Book Belongs to:

Name

Age

Coloring Book with Cute Animals

Bev BOBSON

Copyright Page

Cat

Rabbit

Puppy

Squirrel

Tiger

Duckling

Elephant

Bunnies

Pony

Sparrow

Dog

Teddy Bear

Dog

Bee

Rabbit

Rabbit

Rabbit

Bear

Fisch

Chick

Crocodile

Kangaroo

Deer

Elephant

Mouse

Cat

Lion

Elephant

Bee

Chicken

Dog

Lizard

Octopus

Fish

Bee

Duckling

Fish

Beaver

Sparrow

Pig

Owl

Fish

Pigeon

Ram

Alligator

Sea Horse

Deer

Bee

Mouse

Rooster

Crocodile

Deer

Swan

Beaver

Stork

Ladybug

Monkey

Frog

Walrus

The Panda Bear

Gorilla

Deer

Fox

Ram

Ducklings

Grasshopper

Rabbit

Bear

Rabbit

Cat

Cat

Cat

Cat

Cats

Cat

Frog

Camel

Pigeons

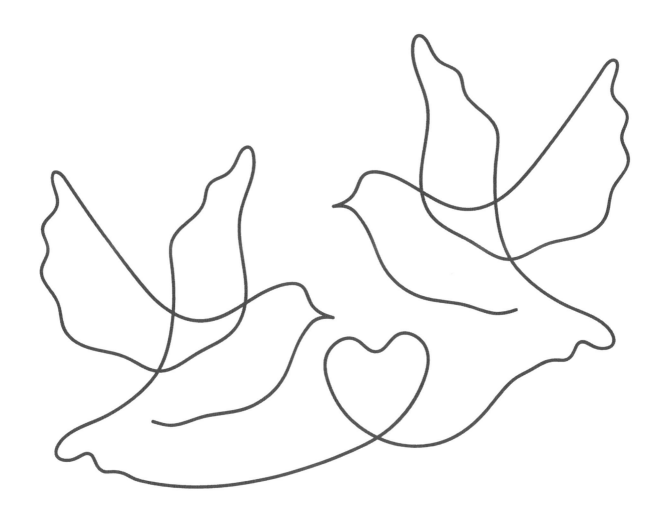

Cat

Cat

Cats

Squirrels

Kitten

Puppy

Dog

Puppy

Kitten

Puppy

Dog

Puppy

Puppy

Cow

Cow

Deer

Swallow

Ram

Deer

Thank You!

Thank you for choosing Coloring Book with Cute Animals! We hope this book has brought joy, creativity, and a sense of wonder to your world. Your support means everything, and we're thrilled to be a part of your artistic journey.

Whether you're relaxing, unwinding, or simply having fun, we hope the adorable animal designs continue to inspire your creativity.

Keep coloring, keep smiling, and keep creating beautiful things!

With heartfelt gratitude,

Bev Bobson

55895849R00057